英文小說解讀攻略

生命篇

戴逸群 —— 主編

陳思安 —— 編著

Ian Fletcher —— 審閱

三民書局

國家圖書館出版品預行編目資料

英文小說解讀攻略：生命篇／戴逸群主編,陳思安編
著.——初版一刷.——臺北市: 三民，2021
　　　面；　　公分.——（閱讀成癮）

　　ISBN 978-957-14-7144-0　（平裝）
　1. 英語 2. 讀本 3. 中等教育

524.38　　　　　　　　　　　　　　110001089

閱讀成癮

英文小說解讀攻略：生命篇

主　　　編	戴逸群
編 著 者	陳思安
審　　　閱	Ian Fletcher
責任編輯	林雅渟
美術編輯	陳奕臻
封面繪圖	Steph Pai

發 行 人	劉振強
出 版 者	三民書局股份有限公司
地　　　址	臺北市復興北路 386 號 (復北門市) 臺北市重慶南路一段 61 號 (重南門市)
電　　　話	(02)25006600
網　　　址	三民網路書店 https://www.sanmin.com.tw

出版日期	初版一刷 2021 年 3 月
書籍編號	S870820
Ｉ Ｓ Ｂ Ｎ	978-957-14-7144-0

三民書局

閱讀成癮

──── 序 ────

　　新課綱強調以「學生」為中心的教與學，注重學生的學習動機與熱情。而英文科首重語言溝通、互動的功能性，培養學生「自主學習」與「終身學習」的能力與習慣。小說「解讀攻略」就是因應新課綱的精神，在「英文小說中毒團隊」的努力下孕育而生。

　　一系列的「解讀攻略」旨在引導學生能透過原文小說的閱讀學習獨立思考，運用所學的知識與技能解決問題；此外也藉由廣泛閱讀進行跨文化反思，提升社會參與並培養國際觀。

　　「英文小說中毒團隊」由普高技高英文老師與大學教授組成，嚴選出主題多樣豐富、適合英文學習的原文小說。我們從文本延伸，設計多元有趣的閱讀素養活動，培養學生從讀懂文本到表達所思的英文能力。團隊秉持著改變臺灣英文教育的使命感，期許我們的努力能為臺灣的英文教育注入一股活水，翻轉大家對英文學習的想像！

戴逸群

──── 作者的話 ────

　　《英文小說解讀攻略：生命篇》帶領讀者一步步走進小說 *13 Reasons Why*，透過 Hannah 與 Clay 等人的視角，解析校園霸凌、身體自主權、自殺、心理健康等極為重要但在日常生活中可能不易討論到的議題。本書不但能幫助讀者有效提升單字量與長篇閱讀理解能力，還能透過多元的學習活動引導讀者探究校園中的重要課題，並將書中所學帶入生活，學會保護自己的生理與心理，減少遺憾發生的可能性。

陳思安

Contents

Picture Credits

All pictures in this publication are authorized for use by Steph Pai and Shutterstock.

《漢娜的遺言》：同理他人的痛苦，成為彼此的祝福

大人常回味青春的美好，可是對正走在青春裡的人們來說，青春有時彷彿一座迷宮，讓人撞得鼻青臉腫。對漢娜‧貝克（Hannah Baker）來說，這座迷宮，沒有出口。

漢娜‧貝克是美國作家傑伊‧艾夏（Jay Asher）的暢銷小說《漢娜的遺言》（13 Reasons Why）裡的主角。讀高中的她，在別人眼裡正值花樣年華，但青春帶給她的，卻是一場帶著摧殘之力的風暴。校園不再是她展現生命力的場所，反成了流言、騷擾、霸凌的溫床，她看不到痛苦的盡頭在哪。

想要結束痛苦的她，最終選擇結束自己的生命。不過她的消失，並非無聲無息。她留下七卷錄音帶，每卷有 A、B 兩面，她錄了十三面的內容，娓娓道出自己走上絕路的十三個原因，各個都是關於她在人際關係中所遭受的背叛與傷害。她也說著這不是單一事件的結果，而是來自多重事件與關係的累積。

2017 年，這部小說被改編成影集，讓這作品再次掀起熱議。而我忘不了當時看完影集的震撼。我對活在複雜與殘酷的人際關係底下，卻無法掙脫的人們感到心疼。漢娜和我們一樣，渴望被認同，渴望有歸屬，但看著她接二連三真心換絕情的故事，實在令人心寒，更跟著她的委屈與難過流下很多眼淚。

另一個看完的感受，就像那部備受好評臺劇的名稱——「我們與惡的距離」，其實一點都不遠，但可怕的是我們可能渾然不覺。也許我們以為那只是無傷大雅的玩笑，以為那不過是場惡作劇，以為別人不會因此受傷……

但聽著漢娜的錄音，我們可以了解到每一次別人的玩笑與漠視，都像一把利刀，在她心上劃出傷痕。很心疼漢娜把她的認同與歸屬給了那些不值得她認同的人。另一方面，那些傷害她的同學們，其實也是受困與迷失的孩子。他們對漢娜的欺騙、背叛、訕笑，可能是他們尋求自保，以獲得同儕認同的姿態。有人也蒙蔽內心真實的感受，只為了得到別人的認同。他們過得也不自由。

青春很難，我們常應和著別人的快樂，而忽略自己的不快樂，或是把自己的快樂建立在對他人的漠視和傷害上。但到頭來，那些傷害都有可能回到自己身上，腐蝕著我們的生命。

《漢娜的遺言》雖然沉重，但讓它努力喚醒我們的感覺與同理心吧！我們能試著去了解漢娜的感受，透過閱讀與理解，去貼近每個渴望愛，但又因為愛而受傷的靈魂。我的經驗告訴我，只要那些感覺能被人了解，我們就多了一點承重之力。每一次的溫柔同理，都會多帶來一絲生存勇氣。如果我們對他人的感受，都是剝削與忽視，我們只是讓彼此都活在無望的悲劇裡。如果我們學會傾聽，開始關心彼此的感受，也願意回應他人的痛苦，第七卷 B 面的空白，就會成為終止悲傷的記號，會是嶄新故事的開始。雖然青春的迷宮有時可能很難走，但我們能用同理傾聽與對話，成為彼此的陪伴與祝福。

諮商心理師　黃柏威

1

Pages 1-4

 Word Power

1. throb *v.* 抽痛
2. kick in 起作用
3. lukewarm *adj.* 不冷不熱的
4. gulp down sth 大口吃或喝

5. serrated *adj.* 鋸齒邊的
6. wastebasket *n.* 廢紙簍
7. collapse *v.* 倒下；崩潰
8. meander *v.* 蜿蜒

 Reading Comprehension

(　　) 1. What is inside the shoebox that the narrator is mailing out in the post office?
　　　　(A) A pair of new shoes.
　　　　(B) A number of tapes.
　　　　(C) Some souvenirs.
　　　　(D) Not mentioned.

(　　) 2. What is most likely the reason that the narrator feels half-asleep?
　　　　(A) It takes him a lot of time and energy to walk to the post office.
　　　　(B) He deals with the tapes overnight.
　　　　(C) He burns the midnight oil studying for a big exam.
　　　　(D) He spends all night trying to figure out who is next on Hannah Baker's list.

(　　) 3. How does the narrator feel about the next recipient?
　　　　(A) Excited.
　　　　(B) Positive.
　　　　(C) Half positive and half negative.
　　　　(D) Negative.

Further Discussion

1. Why does the narrator not wait and send the tapes to the next receiver after school?

_____

_____

_____

_____

_____

_____

2. What is the point of view of this story? What do you think about it? Is it objective and comprehensive?

_____

_____

_____

_____

_____

_____

3. What questions do you have about the narrator and the tapes after you have read the prologue? Write down your questions. They might help you predict what you are going to read in the following chapters.

_____

_____

_____

_____

_____

Observation

Find the descriptions of the narrator's physical actions, feelings, thoughts, imaginings, etc. in the prologue, and draw a picture of him to represent his innermost feelings.

"

"

2

Pages 5–16

 **Word Power**

1. bubble wrap *n.* 氣泡紙
2. scramble *v.* 急速移動
3. go-to *adj.* (為解決某問題) 必找的
4. drape sth over sth 把…蓋在…上
5. spur-of-the-moment *adj.* 一時衝動的
6. varsity *n.* 校隊
7. flake *v.* 剝落
8. bluff *n.* 嚇唬

Reading Comprehension

( ) 1. Why did Hannah make the tapes?
　　(A) To make people remember her.
　　(B) To complete her school project.
　　(C) To explain her suicide.
　　(D) To make a gift for her friends.

( ) 2. How does Hannah make the recipients of the tapes follow her rules?
　　(A) She can't do that because she is dead.
　　(B) If they don't, the copies of the tapes will be released to the public.
　　(C) Someone will command them to listen and pass the package on.
　　(D) She doesn't have to because these friends are loyal to her.

( ) 3. How does Clay confirm that his name is on the list?
　　(A) The names are painted in the corner of Hannah's tapes.
　　(B) He finds a map of the city in his locker.
　　(C) He finds a sticky note attached to the shoebox.
　　(D) Hannah mentions his name in Cassette 1.

1. How does Clay feel when he receives the package? How does he feel after he knows what he is going to hear on the tapes? Try to describe Clay's emotional changes.

   _____

   _____

   _____

   _____

   _____

   _____

2. Following the previous question, find textual evidence that explains Clay's feelings.

   _____

   _____

   _____

   _____

   _____

   _____

3. Why does Clay immediately recognize who Mr. Foley is?

   _____

   _____

   _____

   _____

   _____

   _____

Diary Entry

Imagine yourself as Clay or Hannah. Help them keep a diary that records discovering the tapes (if you were Clay) or having a crush on Justin (if you were Hannah). Try to find the details from the book. Remember to use the past tense.

Memo No. _____

Date   /   /

_____

_____

_____

_____

_____

_____

_____

_____

_____

_____

_____

_____

_____

_____

The picture below is Hannah's map. Mark the locations Hannah mentioned in her tapes while you read the novel. One example (the first red star: Hannah's Old House) has been done for you. Don't forget to come back to the map as you read on.

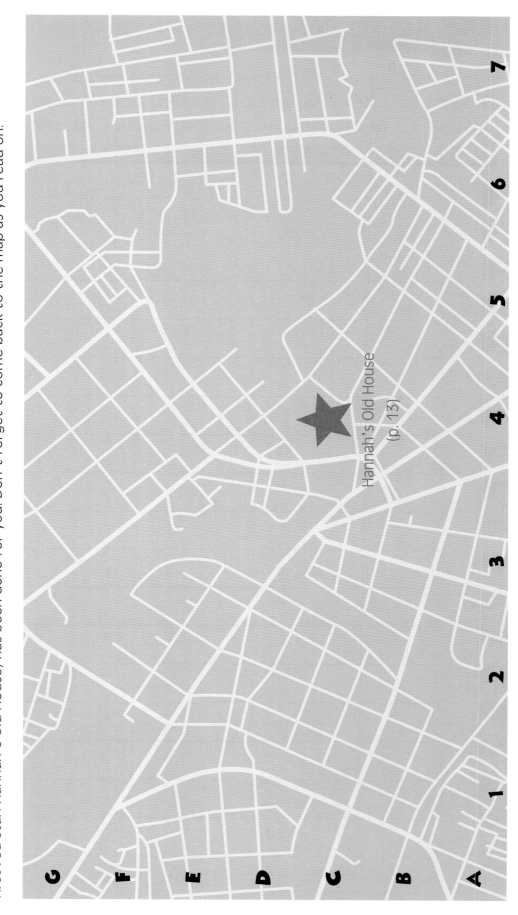

Hannah's Old House (p. 13)

3

Pages 16-35

Word Power

1. contemplate *v.* 沉思
2. steering wheel *n.* 方向盤
3. avert *v.* 轉移 (目光)
4. scowl *v.* 陰沉著臉看

5. pick up on sth 注意到
6. get on sb's nerves 使某人心煩
7. tell me about it 可不是嘛
8. tip sb off 向某人通風報信

Reading Comprehension

( ) 1. How did Hannah get Justin's attention based on her mother's advice about attracting boys?
(A) She wooed him with flowers and gifts.
(B) She flirted with him.
(C) She played hard to get.
(D) She asked him to go out on a date.

( ) 2. How did Hannah feel about Justin? Which of the following statements is **NOT** true?
(A) Hannah wanted to do something sexier after her first kiss with Justin at the park.
(B) There was something about Justin that made her need to be his girlfriend.
(C) She had a freshman crush on Justin and photocopied the schedule of his classes.
(D) She wanted Justin to kiss her at the rocket ship.

( ) 3. On page 30, what do "you" and "this" in "*A rumor based on a kiss made **you** do **this** to yourself?*" refer to?
(A) Justin / listening to the tapes.
(B) Hannah / breaking up with her dream lover.
(C) Hannah / her suicide.
(D) Justin / dating Hannah.

1. Why did Hannah give out her number so cautiously at her new school? What did she do when people asked for her number?

_____

_____

_____

_____

_____

_____

2. What does the snowball effect mean in this chapter? What did it cost Hannah?

_____

_____

_____

_____

_____

_____

3. What is Clay's attitude toward Tony when Tony asks Clay where he is going?

_____

_____

_____

_____

_____

_____

Plot Analysis

Compare and contrast Hannah's first kiss and Clay's first kiss.

Hannah   **Clay**

Who?

When?

Where?

Taste?

How did they feel about the person or the kiss afterwards?

Your comments

4

Pages 36-53

Word Power

1. berserk *adj.* 狂暴的

2. stretch the truth 言過其實

3. repercussion *n.* 負面影響；惡果

4. traumatic *adj.* 造成精神創傷的

5. sweet tooth *n.* 嗜甜

6. mesmerize *v.* 迷惑住

7. condescending *adj.* 居高臨下的

8. agonizingly *adv.* 折磨人地

Reading Comprehension

(　　) 1. According to Hannah, each event on these tapes might not have happened without someone's action. What was it?

(A) Wally selling candy bars.

(B) Jimmy taking a sneaky peek.

(C) Alex making the list.

(D) Jessica taking her revenge.

(　　) 2. What might have made Hannah's classmates change the way they saw someone in school?

(A) Rumors.

(B) The WHO'S HOT / WHO'S NOT list.

(C) The Best Lips category on the list.

(D) All of the above.

(　　) 3. Who did Hannah think was responsible for her being harassed?

(A) Wally.

(B) Justin Foley.

(C) Jimmy Long.

(D) Alex Standall.

YOU ARE LOVED

Further Discussion

1. To Hannah, what was the topic of CASSETTE 1: SIDE B? Find textual evidence in the chapter.

_____

_____

_____

_____

_____

_____

2. What was the repercussion of the WHO'S HOT / WHO'S NOT list mentioned on the tape?

_____

_____

_____

_____

_____

_____

3. Hannah was harassed by the nameless boy. What would you do if you were harassed the same way?

_____

_____

_____

_____

_____

_____

Dealing with Bullying

Bullying can come in different forms. Please check the items in the table below that describe what you observed happening to Hannah, and then answer the following two questions.

Verbal bullying

Saying unkind things to Hannah or writing mean words about her.

- ☐ ① Laughing at Hannah.
- ☐ ② Making improper comments and gossiping about Hannah's first kiss.
- ☐ ③ Making unkind remarks about Hannah.
- ☐ ④ Threatening to cause physical harm to Hannah.

Social bullying

Doing things to damage Hannah's reputation or relationships with other people.

- ☐ ① Isolating Hannah deliberately.
- ☐ ② Forbidding other people to make friends with Hannah.
- ☐ ③ Spreading rumors about Hannah.
- ☐ ④ Embarrassing Hannah in class.

1. What do you see in the nameless boy in the chapter? How would you describe him?

2. What would you do if you saw someone being bullied?

5

Pages 54-68

Word Power

1. kick in 開始

2. new-student orientation *n.* 新生訓練

3. psychobabble *n.* 心理學術語的賣弄

4. blindside *v.* 出其不意地打擊

5. montage *n.* 蒙太奇(一種電影剪輯的手法)

6. peel away 分道揚鑣

7. haven *n.* 安全的地方

8. get back at someone 向某人報復

Reading Comprehension

( ) 1. Which of the following statements is **NOT** true?

    (A) Neither Jessica nor Hannah wanted Ms. Antilly to arrange such a meeting for them.

    (B) This was the first time Ms. Antilly had tried to match up friends.

    (C) It turned out that Hannah and Jessica spent time hanging out after this student orientation.

    (D) Hannah, Jessica, and Alex formed a circle of trust that lasted a pretty long time.

( ) 2. What was the souvenir that Jessica left Hannah with after their fight at Monet's?

    (A) A picture.   (B) A receipt for their drinks.

    (C) A bruise.   (D) A tiny scar.

( ) 3. According to Hannah, what might be the reason that Jessica got mad at Hannah?

    (A) Hannah got "Best Lips in the Freshman Class" on Alex's list.

    (B) Jessica got "Worst Lips in the Freshman Class" on Alex's list.

    (C) Jessica believed that the rumors about Hannah and Alex were true.

    (D) Jessica needed to blame someone in order to release her anger after she stopped being friends with Hannah.

Further Discussion

1. How did Hannah judge her relationship with Jessica and Alex? Why do you think their relationship could not last long?

_____
_____
_____
_____
_____
_____

2. Why did Hannah think those rumors "needed to be true" for Jessica? Why would Jessica rather believe in the rumors than Hannah?

_____
_____
_____
_____
_____
_____

3. How did Jessica hurt Hannah physically and mentally? What did she do to Hannah?

_____
_____
_____
_____
_____
_____

Hannah's Emotional Range

The quality of Hannah's friendship with Alex and Jessica fluctuated over time. Try to draw the emotional range and describe how Hannah felt.

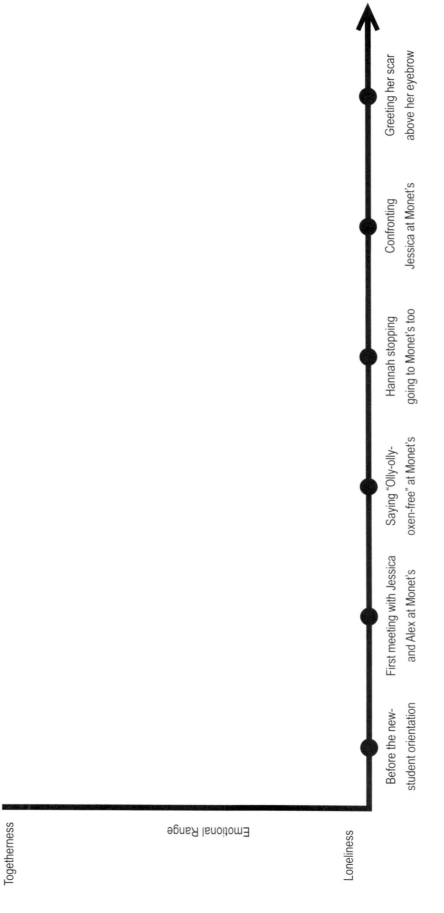

Emotional Range

Togetherness

Loneliness

Before the new-
student orientation

First meeting with Jessica
and Alex at Monet's

Saying "Olly-olly-
oxen-free" at Monet's

Hannah stopping
going to Monet's too

Confronting
Jessica at Monet's

Greeting her scar
above her eyebrow

17

Events	Hannah's feelings
Before the new-student orientation (pp. 55–56)	Hannah didn't want to attend the new-student orientation proposed by Ms. Antilly as Hannah was worried that many things could go wrong.
First meeting with Jessica and Alex at Monet's	
Saying "Olly-olly-oxen-free" at Monet's	
Hannah stopping going to Monet's too	
Confronting Jessica at Monet's	
Greeting her scar above her eyebrow	

6

Pages 69–92

Word Power

1. muffled *adj.* 聲音模糊、低沉的
2. Peeping Tom *n.* 偷窺者
3. lash out at sb (突然) 狠打；斥責
4. the initiative *n.* 主動權

5. Goody Two-Shoes *n.* 假正經的人
6. sneak *v.* 悄悄地走
7. validate *v.* 證實
8. ad-lib *v.* 講話時臨場發揮

Reading Comprehension

(   ) 1. What made Hannah think someone was snapping photos of her?
    (A) She saw a shadow in the moonlight.
    (B) She heard footsteps by the window.
    (C) She heard a sound that a camera makes.
    (D) She heard a kick on the wall.

(   ) 2. Whom did Hannah talk to about the Peeping Tom outside her bedroom?
    (A) Her parents.
    (B) Kat.
    (C) Jessica.
    (D) A girl at school whose name Hannah did not mention.

(   ) 3. What does Clay find in the scribble book at Monet's?
    (A) The words: Everyone needs an olly-olly-oxen-free.
    (B) Three sets of initials.
    (C) A picture of Hannah wrapping her arm around Courtney.
    (D) All of the above.

YOU ARE LOVED **Further Discussion**

1. Why did Hannah talk to the girl sitting in front of her and invite her over to catch the Peeping Tom? Find textual evidence.

_____
_____
_____
_____
_____
_____

2. Why did Hannah think it was Tyler Down that stalked her and took pictures of her?

_____
_____
_____
_____
_____
_____

3. How did Tyler's shots affect Hannah? How did Hannah feel about Tyler's unacceptable behavior?

_____
_____
_____
_____
_____
_____

Music Appreciation—"Thriller"

🔲 SCAN ME

📽 Michael Jackson — "Thriller"

"Thriller" is a very popular song by Michael Jackson, and the scary atmosphere it presents matches Hannah's story in this chapter. Answer the following questions.

1. Search the Internet and read the lyrics first. What do you think "thriller" refers to in the song?

2. What part of the song do you think may correspond to Hannah's creepy experience when she stayed home alone?

"Thriller" lyrics	What happened to Hannah
Something evil's lurking in the dark	. . . I knew someone was standing outside. (p. 80)

3. What a "thriller" scene look like differs from person to person. What is your "thriller" scene? Write down at least one example.

7

Pages 93-104

 Word Power

1. sink in (某事) 被漸漸明白
2. groom *v.* 培養
3. anthology *n.* 精選集
4. bat *v.* 眨眼
5. tumble *v.* 下沉
6. compelled *adj.* 有必要的
7. buckle up 繫上安全帶
8. valedictorian *n.* 畢業典禮上致詞的畢業生代表

 Reading Comprehension

( ) 1. Did Hannah think Courtney was sweet and nice when she recorded the tapes?
   (A) Yes.
   (B) No.
   (C) Sometimes.
   (D) Not given.

( ) 2. Who was Hannah giving a back massage when Tyler peeked from the outside?
   (A) Courtney.
   (B) Jessica.
   (C) Kat.
   (D) Not mentioned.

( ) 3. Why did Hannah put Courtney on the tapes?
   (A) Because she was good at massaging Hannah's back.
   (B) Because Hannah was jealous of Courtney's sweet personality.
   (C) Because she used Hannah and was not a genuine person.
   (D) Because she was Hannah's best friend.

Further Discussion

1. Describe Courtney's appearance and characteristics.

_____
_____
_____
_____
_____
_____

2. Why does Clay think Courtney hearing her story on the tapes must have "killed her"?

_____
_____
_____
_____
_____
_____

3. How did Courtney treat Hannah after the Peeping Tom incident? What did Hannah think about Courtney's reactions?

_____
_____
_____
_____
_____
_____

Illustration—Courtney and Hannah

Draw the characters—Courtney and Hannah—and the scenes of their interactions. Think about what they said and thought. Here are some guided questions: 1. How did Courtney and Hannah's relationship start? 2. How did Courtney treat Hannah? 3. What was Courtney's plan for the party? As there are no right or wrong answers, feel free to use your imagination and creativity.

24

8

Pages 104–118

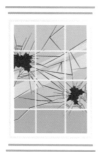

 Word Power

1. stifle *v.* 壓抑
2. backfire *v.* 適得其反
3. egg sb on 慫恿
4. amnesia *n.* 健忘，失憶

5. well *v.* (液體) 湧出
6. chauffeur *n.* 私人司機
7. fiddle with (因緊張或無聊) 用手指撥弄
8. prowl *v.* 潛行，徘徊

Reading Comprehension

(　) 1. Which of the following statements is true regarding the person Clay encounters on the bus?
　　　(A) That person is Courtney Crimsen.
　　　(B) That person always dresses in fancy clothes.
　　　(C) Clay had a crush on that person back in ninth grade.
　　　(D) Clay has not talked to that person for a while.

(　) 2. Who refuses to throw a rock at Tyler's window?
　　　(A) Clay.
　　　(B) Alex.
　　　(C) Marcus.
　　　(D) All of the above.

(　) 3. Why did the unnamed cute guy approach Hannah at the party?
　　　(A) Because Courtney sent him over to talk to Hannah.
　　　(B) Because he wanted to rescue Hannah from being bothered by Tyler.
　　　(C) Because he overheard Courtney gossiping about Hannah's dresser drawers.
　　　(D) Because he thought Hannah looked pretty.

Further Discussion

1. State the reasons why Courtney invited Hannah to go to the party. How did Courtney view Hannah?

_____

_____

_____

_____

_____

_____

2. How did Hannah realize that she was playing the role of a chauffeur the night of the party?

_____

_____

_____

_____

_____

_____

3. What happened at the party that made Hannah learn again about the negative consequences of someone's actions?

_____

_____

_____

_____

_____

_____

Imagine yourself as Courtney and Hannah. What would you think at these different times? Speak for them. One example has been done for you.

Courtney

Hannah

After the Peeping Tom's visit

- Hannah thinks I am sweet and nice. She is like everyone else. I don't need to say hello and goodbye to her more often than I say to other people.

- Courtney and I are more than just casual acquaintances. How can she leave without saying goodbye after class? This feels intentional. (p. 97)

Before the party

During the party

9

Pages 119-148

 Word Power

1. fallback *adj.* 備用的，應變的
2. backpedal *v.* 收回意見；改變立場
3. nosy *adj.* 好管閒事的
4. shrug sth off 對某事滿不在乎

5. wary *adj.* 謹慎的
6. frame of mind 心態
7. endgame *n.* 最後階段
8. pry *v.* 掰開，撬開

 Reading Comprehension

(　) 1. Where could students get the results of their Oh My Dollar Valentines?
　　(A) At the student body office.
　　(B) On the internet.
　　(C) Through their email.
　　(D) Not mentioned.

(　) 2. With whom did the survey match Hannah?
　　(A) Holden Caulfield.
　　(B) Clay Jensen.
　　(C) Marcus Cooley.
　　(D) Zach Dempsey.

(　) 3. Who does Clay think the cheerleader was in this chapter?
　　(A) Courtney Crimsen.
　　(B) Jessica Davis.
　　(C) Jenny Kurtz.
　　(D) Not mentioned.

Further Discussion

1. Why did Hannah agree to meet Marcus at Rosie's Diner when she knew Marcus hung out with Alex, who she no longer trusted?

_____
_____
_____
_____
_____
_____

2. What did Hannah decide the next day? Why did she make such a decision?

_____
_____
_____
_____
_____
_____

3. Hannah thought she was the only one who cared about herself. In fact, it was not true. Find out how Clay has been admiring and caring about Hannah in the chapter.

_____
_____
_____
_____
_____

 **Soul Mate Survey**

Many people believe that there is one right person, a soul mate, for everyone. Whether you believe in soul mates or not, it is true that many people long for love to some degree. Now let's design a survey about soul mates. Fill in the charts below.

About Yourself

What things or features do you value when looking for a partner? Tick the box, or come up with new ideas. Share with the class why you think they are important.

☐ gender   ☐ religion

☐ education   ☐ height/weight

☐ age   ☐ occupation

☐ dress style   ☐ diet

☐ political views   ☐ personality

☐ hobbies   ☐ health status

☐ family background   ☐ financial status

Other:

_____

_____

Soul Mate Survey

Complete the survey template in your own words. (It can tell people what you value.)

(5=strongly agree, 4=agree, 3=neutral, 2=disagree, 1=strongly disagree)

Statements	5	4	3	2	1
1. I believe I will find my soul mate.	☐	☐	☐	☐	☐
2. My soul mate is a person who _____ _____ (definition of soul mates)	☐	☐	☐	☐	☐
3. I value _____ most in my soul mate. (the most important quality)	☐	☐	☐	☐	☐
4. When I am with my soul mate, I can _____ _____	☐	☐	☐	☐	☐
5. My soul mate will make me feel _____ _____	☐	☐	☐	☐	☐
6. When we quarrel, _____ _____ _____	☐	☐	☐	☐	☐
7. When I find my soul mate, I hope he or she has gone through several relationships before we find each other.	☐	☐	☐	☐	☐

◆ Invite some people to fill out your survey and see if there are any interesting results.

◆ Compare and contrast your opinions about soul mates and share with the class.

10

Pages 149–173

Hannah

Word Power

1. catch one's breath 喘口氣
2. elective *n.* 選修課
3. snicker *v.* 竊笑
4. anonymously *adv.* 匿名地

5. sarcastic *adj.* 挖苦的
6. telltale *adj.* 洩漏祕密的
7. crumple sth up 把…揉成一團
8. chime in 插話附和

Reading Comprehension

(　　) 1. What does Clay think of Peer Communications class?
    (A) It is easy to pass.
    (B) It is a fun class.
    (C) It is his safe haven.
    (D) It is helpful in relieving stress.

(　　) 2. What do students owe Mrs. Bradley if they snicker at what others say in her class?
    (A) A detention.
    (B) A dollar.
    (C) An extra bag notes of encouragement.
    (D) A chocolate bar.

(　　) 3. Who probably witnessed what happened between Marcus and Hannah at Rosie's Diner?
    (A) Justin Foley.
    (B) Zach Dempsey.
    (C) Alex Standall.
    (D) Tyler Down.

1. What did Mrs. Bradley devise for her students to encourage them to say what they felt? Why would she do so?

_____

_____

_____

_____

_____

_____

2. In this chapter, Hannah talked about what happened at Rosie's Diner and in Peer Communications class. How do these two events connect?

_____

_____

_____

_____

_____

_____

3. In this chapter, what warning signs of suicidal behavior did Hannah show?

_____

_____

_____

_____

_____

_____

Hannah said she felt more and more like an outcast. If you were her classmate, what would you say to encourage her? Write some notes to let her feel cared about.

Hannah,
I am sorry about those rumors.
You don't deserve that.

Like your new haircut.
Sorry I didn't tell you sooner.

☺

11

Pages 174–193

Word Power

1. stand-in *n.* 替代
2. decipher *v.* 破解
3. come to light 披露、真相大白
4. vouch for sth/sb 為…擔保
5. flinch *v.* 猛然一顫；退縮
6. fess up 坦白
7. get under sb's skin 激怒某人
8. escapade *n.* 冒險的、越軌的行為

Reading Comprehension

(　) 1. What did the person who showed Hannah how to appreciate poetry tell her?
　　(A) That she can see poetry as a puzzle.
　　(B) That the readers can decode the words based on their life experiences.
　　(C) That poetry is the best way to explore one's emotions.
　　(D) All of the above.

(　) 2. Why did Hannah stop writing poems?
　　(A) Because she decided to try something else to make herself happy.
　　(B) Because the poetry class she took was such a disappointment.
　　(C) Because she no longer wanted to know herself.
　　(D) Because she lost her spiral notebook and didn't want to buy a new one.

(　) 3. Who is Mr. Editor?
　　(A) Ryan Shaver.
　　(B) Justin Foley.
　　(C) Marcus Cooley.
　　(D) Zach Dempsey.

1. Clay did not believe he should be on the list before. Why does he think otherwise now?

_____

_____

_____

_____

_____

_____

_____

2. How did Ryan analyze Hannah's poem that she wrote after the discussion of suicide in Peer Communications class?

_____

_____

_____

_____

_____

_____

3. What did Hannah think of the poem-stealing incident?

_____

_____

_____

_____

_____

_____

Poetry Writing

Read Hannah's first poem below and circle the words that rhyme. Use her poem as a model format and finish your own poem in rhyme. Then, ask your classmates for their opinions of your poem.

If my love were an ocean,

there would be no more land.

If my love were a desert,

you would see only sand.

If my love were a star—

late at night, only light.

And if my love could grow wings,

I'd be soaring in flight.

If my love were _____

there would be _____

If my love were _____

you would see only _____

If my love were _____

_____, _____

And if my love could _____

I'd _____

12

Pages 194–207

Word Power

1. the remainder *n.* 剩餘部分
2. stellar *adj.* 傑出的
3. wait in the wings 準備就緒
4. come to grips with sth
   理解並著手處理

5. grounded *adj.* 被禁足的
6. the calm before the storm 暴風雨前的寧靜
7. detour *n.* 繞路
8. silhouette *n.* 輪廓；剪影

Reading Comprehension

( ) 1. Which of the following statements is **NOT** true?
   (A) Tony follows Clay out of curiosity.
   (B) Tony has the second set of tapes.
   (C) Clay's tape is the fifth tape.
   (D) Tony insists that Clay should keep listening.

( ) 2. Why does Tony ask Clay to get in his car?
   (A) Because he needs to make sure everyone on the list follows Hannah's instructions.
   (B) Because he wants to take his Walkman back from Clay.
   (C) Because he is hungry and wants to have dinner at Rosie's Diner.
   (D) Because he wants to give Clay a ride home.

( ) 3. Why did Hannah go to the party?
   (A) Because Hannah happened to be in the neighborhood when she went to visit the house she used to live in.
   (B) Because Clay would be there, and Hannah wanted to talk to him.
   (C) Because Hannah wanted to have a head-on confrontation with Jessica.
   (D) Because Hannah wanted to break her parents' rule.

Further Discussion

1. Hannah said the tapes give the reasons why her life ended. Yet, if Hannah did not think Clay belonged on the list, why did she put him on the tapes?

_____

_____

_____

_____

_____

_____

2. When Hannah stood in front of her old house, what was the feeling that overwhelmed her and stayed with her all night? What did Hannah realize?

_____

_____

_____

_____

_____

_____

3. What did Hannah mean by "Everything . . . affects everything" on page 201? Do you agree with her?

_____

_____

_____

_____

_____

_____

Character Word Cloud

Come up with at least ten words or phrases related to Clay Jensen, whether they are about his thoughts, personality traits, behaviors, feelings, or his reputation. Then, use these words to create a word cloud portraying Clay. The word cloud can be an image or a symbol that you think can represent him.

Words	Textual Evidence
angry / bitter / sorrowful	Clay's voice shakes when he talks to Marcus outside Tyler's house. He grips the rock harder and tries to hold back tears. (p. 109)

13

Pages 208-219

 **Word Power**

1. catch sb off guard 使某人措手不及
2. out of the blue 出乎意料地
3. intrusive *adj.* 唐突的；打擾的
4. off limits *adj.* 禁止的
5. wind up 最後來到
6. clasp *v.* 緊抓、緊搗
7. intrigued *adj.* 被迷住的
8. bypass *v.* 繞過

Reading Comprehension

( ) 1. How did Clay react when he first saw Hannah at the party?
  (A) He greeted Hannah and talked to her.
  (B) He greeted Hannah but did not try to start a conversation.
  (C) He panicked and went out through the gate.
  (D) He panicked but still forced a smile.

( ) 2. Who shared the same couch with Hannah and Clay at the party?
  (A) Marcus Cooley and an unknown girl.
  (B) Jessica Davis and Justin Foley.
  (C) Jessica Davis and Alex Standall.
  (D) Courtney Crimsen and Zach Dempsey.

( ) 3. Which of the following statements is true about Clay when he finishes listening to his tape?
  (A) He cries alone in Tony's car.
  (B) He does not understand his role in this tape.
  (C) He takes comfort from the fact that he was there for Hannah that night.
  (D) He now understands why Hannah would react the way she did that night.

1. What was Hannah's inner struggle when she and Clay talked about heavy topics at the party?

_____
_____
_____
_____
_____
_____

2. What do you think was the turning point for Hannah that night of the party? What might have been the unexpected twist that ruined Hannah's night with Clay?

_____
_____
_____
_____
_____
_____

3. Why do you think Clay says that he never really missed Hannah until now?

_____
_____
_____
_____
_____

In Hannah's Shoes

Have you ever had a crush on someone? Now imagine you were Hannah and try to put yourself in her shoes. Let's help her sort out her feelings that night. (1) Come up with at least another three positive and negative words or phrases that describe Hannah's feelings and put them in their respective categories. (2) Write down your comments.

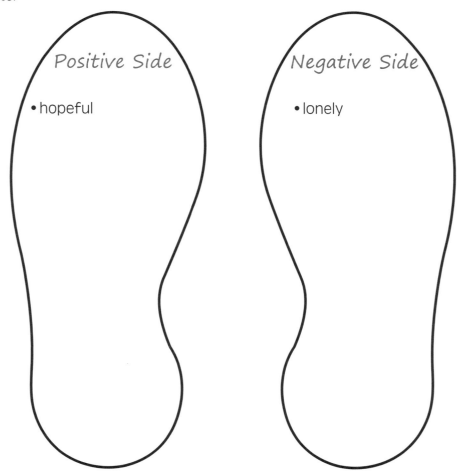

Positive Side
• hopeful

Negative Side
• lonely

Comments about the positive side	Comments about the negative side

44

14

Pages 220-231

Word Power

1. stumble *v.* 跌跌撞撞地走
2. tuck sb in 幫某人蓋被子
3. voyeuristic *adj.* 偷窺的
4. hazardous *adj.* 危險的
5. dawn on sb 使某人明白
6. meltdown *n.* 崩潰
7. revolve around 以⋯為中心
8. swap *v.* 交換

Reading Comprehension

( ) 1. Whose stories take up two sides of Hannah's tapes?
   (A) Clay Jensen's.
   (B) Justin Foley's.
   (C) Jessica Davis'.
   (D) Jenny Kurtz's.

( ) 2. Who does Clay think the nameless boy who said "Just relax" is?
   (A) Bryce Walker.
   (B) Justin Foley.
   (C) Marcus Cooley.
   (D) Not mentioned.

( ) 3. Who might never know she was raped at the party until she listened to Hannah's tapes?
   (A) Courtney Crimsen.
   (B) Ms. Antilly.
   (C) Jenny Kurtz.
   (D) Jessica Davis.

1. Why couldn't Hannah leave the room after Clay took off?

_____

_____

_____

_____

_____

_____

2. What did Hannah think of Justin's action?

_____

_____

_____

_____

_____

_____

_____

3. What did Hannah think or feel when she went through the horrible night with the poor girl? What impact did this incident have on Hannah?

_____

_____

_____

_____

_____

_____

_____

Dos and Don'ts

Despite the fact that the events in this chapter are difficult to read about and process, it is essential for us to learn how to prevent dating violence and sexual assault from happening and learn what to do if it were to happen. Write down at least another three dos and don'ts for each category.

How to stop dating violence and sexual assault before it starts	
Dos	**Don'ts**
• Always respect yourself and others. • Get your own drinks and always keep sight of your drinks.	• Don't have alcoholic drinks. • Don't share drinks with others.

Tips to help someone who has been through dating violence or sexual assault	
Dos	**Don'ts**
• Believe and support them. • Listen to them and show acceptance.	• Don't be judgmental. • Don't blame the victims.

15

Pages 232–252

Word Power

1. pull oneself together 冷靜下來
2. glaze over (眼神) 呆滯
3. scroll *v.* 滑動
4. knot *v.* 打結

5. stagger *v.* 踉蹌地走
6. dent *n.* 凹痕
7. warp *v.* 彎曲變形
8. collide *v.* 相撞

Reading Comprehension

( ) 1. Which of the following is the suicidal warning sign Hannah showed in this chapter?
(A) She gave her bike to Tony.
(B) She told Tony she would like to end her own life.
(C) She gave Tony a collection of her tapes.
(D) She said she would leave the town for good.

( ) 2. Clay believes that Hannah's mind was made up by the time she went to visit Tony. What does this mean?
(A) That Hannah had decided to forget all the bad things and move on.
(B) That Hannah had decided to transfer to another school.
(C) That Hannah had decided to move to another town.
(D) That Hannah had decided to commit suicide.

( ) 3. Who is the cheerleader in the student body office who gave Hannah the results of her Oh My Dollar Valentines survey?
(A) Jessica Davis.
(B) Jenny Kurtz.
(C) Courtney Crimsen.
(D) Skye Miller.

1. Why does Clay say "thank you" to Tony? What does he thank Tony for?

_____

_____

_____

_____

_____

_____

2. What did the night of the party mean to Hannah? What did the two things that happened that night lead her to think about?

_____

_____

_____

_____

_____

_____

3. What do you think of Hannah's attempts to stop Jenny from driving away?

_____

_____

_____

_____

_____

About Teen Suicide

Right after Tony learned about Hannah's intention of committing suicide, he tried to reach out to Hannah, but it was too late. Throughout the chapters, what warning signs of suicide did Hannah show? Draw lines to Hannah's icon from the warning signs you have noticed and give textual evidence from the text to support your answers.

Teens' Suicidal Warning Signs

- 1. Discussing or thinking about suicide and death.
  → **when in Peer Communications class (p. 169)**
- 2. Predicting one's departure.

- 3. Talking about feeling hopeless, helpless, depressed, guilty, etc.
- 4. Going through extreme mood swings.

- 5. Isolating oneself from friends or family.

- 6. Writing notes, poems, or letters about death, not being accepted, etc.
- 7. Giving away personal belongings.

- 8. Losing interest in doing one's favorite activities.

- 9. Having trouble concentrating or focusing.

- 10. Not caring about schoolwork, which worsens one's grades.
- 11. Having major changes in daily habits.

- 12. Starting to take unnecessary risks or acting out.

- 13. Using drugs or alcohol.

- 14. Changing one's appearance suddenly.

16

Pages 253-267

 Word Power

1. preconditioned *adj.* 具備…先決條件
2. house-sit *v.* 替人看家
3. barf *v.* 嘔吐
4. blast *v.* 發出巨響
5. sober up 醒酒，清醒
6. coincidence *n.* 巧合
7. after-party *n.* 派對結束後的社交活動
8. inviting *adj.* 吸引人的

 Reading Comprehension

( ) 1. Hannah had been struggling to say a certain word, but in this chapter, she finally said it. What is the word?
    (A) Illness.
    (B) Rape.
    (C) Suicide.
    (D) Ending.

( ) 2. Where is Clay heading when he listens to this tape?
    (A) A gas station.
    (B) Courtney's house.
    (C) Eisenhower Park.
    (D) Hannah's house.

( ) 3. Why did Hannah join Courtney and Bryce and rest in the hot tub?
    (A) Because she wanted to sober up after the party.
    (B) Because she would like to fix her friendship with both of them.
    (C) Because she needed to relax her tense muscles.
    (D) Because she wanted to make use of the circumstances to let go of herself.

Further Discussion

1. What did Hannah think and decide while she was making the tape for Bryce Walker? What are your reflections on this tape?

_____

_____

_____

_____

_____

_____

2. Why does Clay think Hannah should not have joined Courtney's after-party with Bryce Walker?

_____

_____

_____

_____

_____

_____

3. Hannah specified she was using Bryce and that she did not say no or push him away. What do you think about the hot-tub incident and her explanation?

_____

_____

_____

_____

_____

_____

Character Log

Find descriptions of the three characters in this tape, whether they are about their thoughts, actions, or personality, and write them down.

Hannah	• calm, content (p. 253) • giving up on herself (p. 253)
Courtney	
Bryce	

17

Pages 268~280

 Word Power

1. scoot *v.* (坐著) 挪動
2. conspiracy *n.* 密謀
3. pop/come out of the woodwork 冒了出來
4. confidential *adj.* 保密的
5. blunt *adj.* 直截了當的
6. move on 接受現實、往前進
7. get over sth 從某事當中恢復過來；忘記創傷
8. get on with sth 開始 (或繼續) 做某事

 Reading Comprehension

(　) 1. Who did Hannah talk to when she was giving life one last try?
(A) Bryce Walker.　　　　　(B) Mr. Porter.
(C) Justin Foley.　　　　　(D) Zach Dempsey.

(　) 2. How is Cassette 7: Side A different from what Clay has heard in the previous tapes?
(A) It tells Hannah's background story before she moved to this town.
(B) Hannah's tone is optimistic while her tone before was sad and bitter.
(C) It is about an adult outside the school.
(D) It is an actual recording of Hannah's conversation with someone.

(　) 3. Hannah told Mr. Porter that she got what she came for. What did Hannah figure out?
(A) That nobody liked her.
(B) That she could move beyond what had happened to her.
(C) That she had made her intention clear, but people did not care enough.
(D) That even if she pressed charges, it wouldn't matter much.

Further Discussion

1. Why did Hannah go to Mr. Porter's office? What was her purpose? How did it turn out?

_____

_____

_____

_____

_____

_____

2. What do you think was the effect of Mr. Porter's advice on Hannah?

_____

_____

_____

_____

_____

_____

3. Do you think Mr. Porter was a competent guidance counselor? Why or why not?

_____

_____

_____

_____

_____

If there is a website for Mr. Porter's English class, what will it be like? If Mr. Porter posts a question, what comments may his students leave? Write comments for Hannah, yourself, and two other characters you choose. Then, draw the profile photos.

Mr. Porter's English Class

Private Group

About

Discussion

Members

Events

➤ School Dance
Buy your ticket before March 1st!

➤ Student-Counselor Meetings
Make an appointment anytime you need to talk to someone.

Videos

Photos

Files

Shakespeare 101 handouts

Booklist for this semester

Search this group

Mr. Porter

How would you define friendship?

Leave your comment below before next Monday, and we will discuss this topic in class.

👍 12   💬 4

Hannah Baker

.... Like - Reply

_____

.... Like - Reply

_____

.... Like - Reply

_____ (your name)

.... Like - Reply

18

Pages 281–288

 Word Power

1. spool *n.* 捲軸
2. podium *n.* 演講臺
3. profoundly *adv.* 極度地
4. freestanding *adj.* 獨立式的

5. custodian *n.* 管理員
6. crumble *v.* 粉碎
7. motion *v.* 做手勢；點頭示意
8. stretch *n.* 一段

 Reading Comprehension

(　　) 1. To whom did Clay miss the chance to talk to on the bus the night before?
　　　(A) Skye Miller.
　　　(B) Steve Oliver.
　　　(C) Zach Dempsey.
　　　(D) Mr. Porter.

(　　) 2. What does Clay feel when he casts a glance into Mr. Porter's room?
　　　(A) Pain and anger.
　　　(B) Sadness and pity.
　　　(C) Hope.
　　　(D) All of the above.

(　　) 3. Who is the next recipient of Hannah's tapes after Clay?
　　　(A) Mr. Porter.
　　　(B) Jenny Kurtz.
　　　(C) Hannah's parents.
　　　(D) Not mentioned.

1. Clay has never been this late for class until today. Why?

   _____

   _____

   _____

   _____

   _____

   _____

2. Does Clay change in any way? How? What does Clay do for Skye after he listens to the tapes?

   _____

   _____

   _____

   _____

   _____

   _____

3. What do you think Clay can say to Skye to start a conversation with her? List some conversation starters.

   _____

   _____

   _____

   _____

   _____

   _____

Book Critic

Congratulations on finishing *13 Reasons Why*. Now imagine you are a renowned book critic, and your fans are waiting for your review of this book.

My Rating:

1. Introduce the book. What are the themes of this book?

_____

_____

_____

_____

_____

_____

2. Share your favorite part of the novel.

_____

_____

_____

_____

_____

_____

3. Give a recommendation. (E.g., "If you like . . . , you will love this book" or "I recommend this book to anyone who likes . . . .")

_____

_____

_____

_____

_____

_____

13 Reasons Why Not: Personal Happiness List

No one feels good all the time, and sometimes it is just hard to see the bright side. But if we practice identifying what makes us happy, it would be easier to make happiness a choice even in the face of tough situations. Think of 13 things that can bring a smile to your face and make a list.

1	
2	
3	
4	
5	
6	
7	
8	
9	
10	
11	
12	
13	

Carry this personal happiness list with you wherever you go and update it regularly. You will be surprised at the huge difference that it can make to you!

If you could recommend one English song to Hannah that you think may give her some comfort, what song would that be? Write down the title of the song, the name(s) of the singer(s), and the reason why you choose that song. Then, share this song with the class.

Song		Singer(s)	

The reason you recommend this song:

Try to make a compilation of ten good songs to help people regain hope and strength. In addition to the song you recommend above, please collect nine other songs from your classmates to make an album. Then, give this album a title and design a cover.

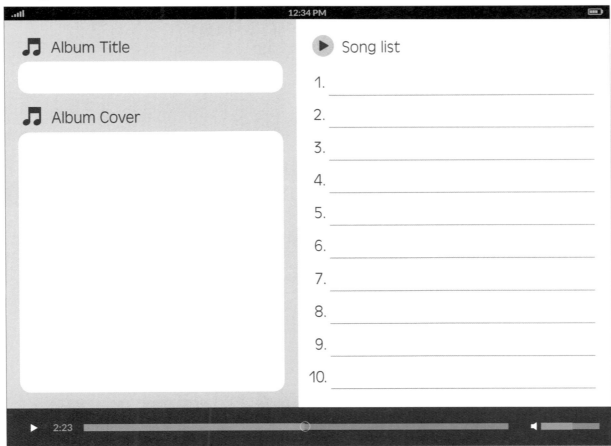

◆ Wonder 解讀攻略

戴逸群 編著／Joseph E. Schier 審閱

Lexile 藍思分級：790

☞ 議題：品德教育、生命教育、家庭教育、閱讀素養

◆ Love, Simon 解讀攻略

戴逸群 主編／林冠瑋 編著／Ian Fletcher 審閱

Lexile 藍思分級：640

☞ 議題：性別平等、人權教育、多元文化、閱讀素養

◆ Matilda 解讀攻略

戴逸群 主編／林佳紋 編著／Joseph E. Schier 審閱

Lexile 藍思分級：840

☞ 議題：性別平等、人權教育、家庭教育、閱讀素養

◆ 英文小說解讀攻略：奇幻篇

戴逸群 主編／簡嘉妤 編著／Ian Fletcher 審閱

Lexile 藍思分級：880

☞ 議題：品德教育、家庭教育、多元文化、閱讀素養

◆ 英文小說解讀攻略：冒險篇

戴逸群 主編／Guy Herring 編著

Lexile 藍思分級：810

☞ 議題：品德教育、家庭教育、科技教育、閱讀素養

Answer Key

Lesson 1
Reading Comprehension
1. (B)   2. (B)   3. (D)

Lesson 2
Reading Comprehension
1. (C)   2. (B)   3. (B)

Lesson 3
Reading Comprehension
1. (C)   2. (A)   3. (C)

Plot Analysis

	Hannah	Clay
Who?	Justin Foley	Andrea Williams
When?	high school freshman	seventh grade, after school
Where?	at Eisenhower Park at the bottom of the slide	behind the gym
Taste?	chili dogs	strawberry lip gloss

Lesson 4
Reading Comprehension
1. (C)   2. (D)   3. (D)

Dealing with Bullying
Verbal bullying: ① ✓, ② ✓, ③ ✓
Social bullying: ③ ✓, ④ ✓

Lesson 5
Reading Comprehension
1. (D)   2. (D)   3. (C)

Lesson 6
Reading Comprehension
1. (C)   2. (D)   3. (D)

Lesson 7
Reading Comprehension
1. (B)   2. (A)   3. (C)

Lesson 8
Reading Comprehension
1. (D)   2. (A)   3. (C)

Lesson 9
Reading Comprehension
1. (A)   2. (C)   3. (C)

Lesson 10
Reading Comprehension
1. (B)   2. (D)   3. (B)

Lesson 11
Reading Comprehension
1. (D)   2. (C)   3. (A)

Poetry Writing
★ land, sand
★ night, light, flight

Lesson 12
Reading Comprehension
1. (A)   2. (A)   3. (B)

Lesson 13
Reading Comprehension
1. (C)   2. (B)   3. (D)

Lesson 14
Reading Comprehension
1. (B)   2. (A)   3. (D)

Lesson 15

Reading Comprehension

1. (A)   2. (D)   3. (B)

About Teen Suicide

1, 4, 5, 6, 7, 10, 14

Lesson 16

Reading Comprehension

1. (C)   2. (C)   3. (D)

Lesson 17

Reading Comprehension

1. (B)   2. (D)   3. (C)

Lesson 18

Reading Comprehension

1. (A)   2. (D)   3. (B)